CUMBRIA LIBRARIES

3 8003 04839 3797

D1585593

This slimy quest
belongs to

THE PROPHECY

Long ago, an evil slug named ZORGOTH tried to eat the entire Super Happy Magic Forest. However, eating a forest is tiring. Zorgoth was overpowered and banished into darkness under a rock. It is said that one day, Zorgoth will return and drink the POTION OF POWER which will grant him the strength to destroy the Super Happy Magic Forest. Only the bravest of heroes will stand against him.

SUPER HAPPY
MAGIC FOREST
SLUG OF DOOM

BY MATTY LONG

OXFORD
UNIVERSITY PRESS

This story begins in the Super Happy Magic Forest,
a place where every day is filled with sunshine,
rainbows, and good times.

But not all good times can last forever . . .

The bravest heroes in the Super Happy Magic Forest were summoned before the Great Council of Happiness.

With their quest clear, the heroes began following the slimy trail of evil.

The trail led the heroes deep below the Super Happy Magic Forest.

It took them across fiery lands
and past hot-tempered foes.

It led them through advanced civilizations, testing their cunning and wit.

With night approaching, the heroes prepared to face
whatever horrors it may bring.

But something didn't seem right.

WHERE'S TREVOR?

Come to think of it, I remember seeing Trevor in a cage back at the Ogre Village...

We have to go back!

With Trevor safe, the heroes continued their race to stop Zorgoth.

Eventually, the heroes arrived at the foot of a great mountain. Somehow, they knew that the Potion of Power must be close.

With Zorgoth defeated, the heroes made the long journey back to the Super Happy Magic Forest.

And when they finally arrived home, there was only one thing left to do . . .

For Nan, Grandpa, and anyone
who enjoyed the first book.

OXFORD
UNIVERSITY PRESS

Great Clarendon Street, Oxford OX2 6DP
Oxford University Press is a department of the University of Oxford.
It furthers the University's objective of excellence in research, scholarship,
and education by publishing worldwide. Oxford is a registered trade mark of
Oxford University Press in the UK and in certain other countries

Text and illustrations copyright © Matty Long 2016
The moral rights of the author and illustrator have been asserted
Database right Oxford University Press (maker)
First published 2016

All rights reserved. No part of this publication may be reproduced,
stored in a retrieval system, or transmitted, in any form or by any means,
without the prior permission in writing of Oxford University Press,
or as expressly permitted by law, or under terms agreed with the appropriate
reprographics rights organization. Enquiries concerning reproduction
outside the scope of the above should be sent to the Rights Department,

Oxford University Press, at the address above
You must not circulate this book in any other binding or cover
and you must impose this same condition on any acquirer

British Library Cataloguing in Publication Data

Data available
ISBN: 978-0-19-274297-1 (hardback)
ISBN: 978-0-19-274298-8 (paperback)
ISBN: 978-0-19-274299-5 (eBook)

1 3 5 7 9 10 8 6 4 2

Printed in China

Paper used in the production of this book is a natural,
recyclable product made from wood grown in sustainable forests.
The manufacturing process conforms to the environmental
regulations of the country of origin.

 # THE LEGEND

And so it was told that thunder crackled and lightning flashed as the five brave heroes fought a terrible battle against the mighty Zorgoth. When nearly all hope was gone, a unicorn with a golden horn rose up and struck a fatal blow. Tales of the unicorn's courage and skill spread across the land. Evil was defeated. A legend was born.